Pearlie Goes to RIO

WENDY HARMER

Illustrated by Gypsy Taylor

RANDOM HOUSE AUSTRALIA

For Miss Maeve — growing her wings
and becoming a beautiful butterfly.
I love to watch you flutter!

A Random House book
Published by Random House Australia Pty Ltd
Level 3, 100 Pacific Highway, North Sydney NSW 2060
www.randomhouse.com.au

First published by Random House Australia in 2014
Copyright © Out of Harms Way Pty Ltd 2014

Addresses for companies within the Random House Group can be found
at www.randomhouse.com.au/offices.

National Library of Australia

Cataloguing-in-Publication Entry
Harmer, Wendy
Pearlie goes to Rio/written by Wendy Harmer;
illustrated by Gypsy Taylor
ISBN: 978 0 85798 216 2 (pbk.)
Series: Harmer, Wendy. Pearlie the park fairy; 16
Target audience: For primary school age
Subjects: Fairies – Juvenile fiction
        Brazil – Juvenile fiction
Other authors/contributors: Taylor, Gypsy

A823.4

Designed and typeset by Kate Barraclough, based on initial series
design by Jobi Murphy
Printed and bound in China by Everbest Printing Ltd

It was a hot and steamy morning when Pearlie the Park Fairy looked out over the wonderful city of Rio de Janeiro.

Queen Emerald's magic ladybird had dropped Pearlie off on the top of a mountain near the city. From there the view almost took her breath away.

'Hurly-burly!' gasped Pearlie.

Away in the distance she could see beautiful beaches with tumbling surf. A little closer were the jumbled white buildings of Rio. And right below her were valleys of deep green rainforest.

'*Vista maravilhosa!*' said a voice behind her. 'Yes! It is a truly marvellous sight.'

Pearlie turned around to see a fairy with a wide smile. She was shading herself with a huge flower umbrella.

'I'm Morena,' said the fairy, as she tossed her shiny black curls. 'And you must be Pearlie. *Bem vinda!* Welcome to Brazil.'

'Why, thank you,' said Pearlie. 'I'm so pleased to be visiting your park.'

Then Pearlie shaded her eyes from the burning sun and looked about.

'Where *is* your park, exactly?' she asked.

'You're in it right now,' laughed Morena. 'Tijuca Forest. This is one of the biggest parks in the world! Now follow me.'

Morena fluttered her lovely wings and zoomed down, down into the leafy forest. The tiny fairy was very fast. She dodged huge tree trunks, bright flowers and even flew under a waterfall.

Pearlie was right behind her.

At last Morena came to a clearing. She pushed aside heavy leaves and thick vines and led Pearlie into a cool, quiet hollow.

'Oooh, it is lovely here,' said Pearlie.

A bright orange beetle scuttled in with a tray of drinks and snacks.

'There is lime or melon juice and *baba de moça* cake. It's made from coconut milk and cream.' Morena said sweetly. 'Eat and drink, Pearlie. You have come to Tijuca Forest just in time for the most exciting night of your life!'

Pearlie nibbled at the cakes and sipped her juice
as Morena told her story.

'The Butterfly Carnival will begin soon and all
the butterflies will parade through the forest.
It is *muito bonito*. That means very beautiful,'
said Morena.

How exciting! Pearlie adored butterflies.
Back home in Jubilee Park she loved to watch
them dance and twirl among the flowers.
And, she had to admit, their wings
were often prettier than her own.

As the afternoon went on, Morena told tales of the strange creatures that could be found in the old forests of Brazil.

There were lizards that walked on water. Bats of the night that ate fish. Massive spiders with stripes like tigers. And even a fish that ate underwater trees!

Pearlie had never heard anything like it.
She was amazed.

'You've travelled a long way,' smiled Morena.
'The sun is going down now, so let's both
sleep. Whatever noises you hear in the night,
remember you are safe with Morena of Tijuca.'

The fairy flitted off and Pearlie fell asleep in a soft bed of moss.

It was still dark when Pearlie was woken by strange sounds she had never heard before.

SWOOSH, SCRABBLE, SNUFFLE, SCRATCH!

The Tijuca rainforest was full of creatures that loved the hot and steamy night.

Pearlie lay awake until the first light of dawn crept into her room. The orange beetle brought her some delicious caramel tarts.

But she wasn't the only one having breakfast.

MUNCH! MUNCH! MUNCH! MUNCH!

'Roots and twigs! What's that sound?'
said Pearlie.

Fairy Morena appeared. '*Bom dia*. Good
morning. That noise is not roots and twigs . . .
it's leaves. It's the caterpillars, and they are very
hungry. Come with me and you will see.' MUNCH!
MUNCH!
MUNCH!
MUNCH.

The two fairies set off.

It was an astonishing sight. Before them was a huge bush. Caterpillars of all shapes and colours covered every leaf. Some had spikes on their backs. Some were covered in feathery spines. Others had long, curly antennae.

And every single one was eating great holes in the green leaves. The caterpillars seemed to be getting fatter by the minute.

'*Caramba!* I have so much to prepare for the carnival. Could you please look after the caterpillars for me today, Pearlie?' asked Morena.

'Of course,' said Pearlie.

'*Obrigada.* Thank you,' said Morena as she flew off. She called over her shoulder, 'And watch out for the hungry birds!'

Pearlie looked about. She could see many beady, birdy eyes in the forest above. The naughty birds were all hoping to make a meal of the caterpillars.

If they did, there would be no butterfly parade.

'Shoo, go away!' called Pearlie. She flitted this way and that, using her wand to zap any bright tail feathers and beaks she could spy.

'AWK, AWK, AWK!' The birds squawked in fright and flapped away through the forest.

Pearlie was very busy all day long.

Not only did the pesky birds keep coming back, but as the caterpillars grew they shed their skins and dropped their old clothes all over the place. Pearlie picked them up and folded them neatly.

The noise of the caterpillars chewing through the leaves was deafening. All day it got louder . . . and louder.

MUNCH, MUNCH, MUNCH, MUNCH!!!

'Phew!' said Pearlie as her wings drooped. 'I do hope they all turn into butterflies soon.'

One by one, the caterpillars stopped eating. They crawled to the underside of the bare branches, where they were safe from the hungry birds. They shed their skins for the very last time.

When Morena returned that evening, all the caterpillars were quiet. They were busy making themselves chrysalises. Inside each chrysalis, a caterpillar would turn into a butterfly.

'*Finalmente!* Finally we will have some peace,' said Morena. 'Now we can prepare our costumes for the carnival. They must be *espetaculares!*'

'Yes,' laughed Pearlie. 'Spectacular.'

The days passed quickly as Pearlie and Morena watched over the chrysalises. They collected feathers and flowers from the forest to make their headdresses, skirts and sandals.

Then Pearlie had a bright idea.

'I think I will use those old caterpillar skins to make a wonderful cloak,' she said.

Morena agreed that would be a very special costume and sure to catch the eye.

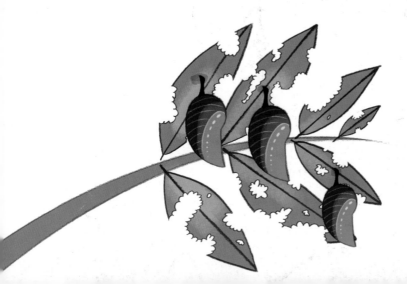

After much sewing, the bright and beautiful cloak was ready. Pearlie put it on and stepped out of the shade to show Morena.

Pearlie twirled and said, 'How do I loo–'

In an instant, a great big greedy parrot swooped down from the branches. It thought Pearlie was a delicious caterpillar treat.

It whisked Pearlie off in its beak and darted through the rainforest.

'EEEEEK,' screeched Pearlie.

In a flash, Morena flew after the hungry bird.

'*Para, para!* Stop, stop!' she shouted.

But the parrot would not stop. Up and up it
flew to the top of the mountain and beyond.
Right up into the cloudless blue sky.

'Help, help!' cried Pearlie.

What could she do? Her wand was tucked in
her bag back at the clearing. The parrot's fierce
beak was crushing her wings. Just one gulp
and she would be gone. Swallowed like a tasty
caramel tart!

ZAP!

Morena's wand gave the parrot's tail feathers a mighty sting.

SQUAAAAAWWK!

The parrot's beak opened and out fell Pearlie. But her wings were crushed and she could not fly.

Down, down from the sky and through the rainforest she tumbled. Past trees. Over waterfalls.

'Huuuuuuuurly-buuuuuuurly!' cried Pearlie.

She was sure to fall on the rocks below.

WHUMP!

Pearlie landed with a bounce on a shimmering . . .
What was it? A flying carpet?

When Pearlie caught her breath, she saw she
had fallen on top of butterfly wings.

A great swarm of baby butterflies had hatched
and flown up the mountain to her rescue.

'*Obrigado*, Miss Pearlie!' they whispered. 'Thank you for looking after us when we were caterpillars!'

'No, no. Thank you,' gasped Pearlie.

The butterflies dropped her gently onto a flower and sang, '*De nada!*' Then they flew off giggling to find a supper of sweet nectar.

'That means "no trouble at all",' said Morena, who was happy to find Pearlie safe and sound. She shuffled her tiny feet.

'You're dancing!' laughed Pearlie.

'It's the samba. The favourite dance of Rio!'
Morena replied as she wiggled some more.
'The butterflies are getting ready, and we will
all be doing the samba at the Butterfly Carnival
tonight.'

That evening, as the sun dropped behind the mountain and the forest fell dark, Pearlie and her new friend admired each other's costumes. They both looked *fantásticas* – although Pearlie had wisely decided to leave her caterpillar cloak behind.

'It is time for the famous Butterfly Carnival of Tijuca to begin,' called Morena.

She waved her wand and a million fairy lights sparkled. A swarm of glittering beetles banged on drums, fat frogs croaked in a booming chorus and the whole rainforest swayed to the samba beat.

Next came a twirling, whirling parade of butterflies. Their wings glowed like brilliant jewels.

In all her life Pearlie had never seen a sight so wonderful.

'This is the best night ever!' she shouted as she danced to the rhythm.

'*Um beijo!* I give you a kiss, dear friend,' said Morena.

'*Muito bom!* Very good,' laughed Pearlie.

Then the little two fairies held hands and danced the night away in the magical rainforest of Tijuca.